First published 1986 by
Walker Books Ltd
184-192 Drummond Street
London NW1 3HP

Text © 1986 Judy Taylor
Illustrations © 1986 Peter Cross

First printed 1986
Reprinted 1986
Printed and bound by L.E.G.O., Vicenza, Italy

British Library Cataloguing in Publication Data
Cross, Peter
Dudley in a jam. – (Dudley the dormouse;4)
I. Title   II. Taylor, Judy   III. Series
823'.914[J]      PZ7

ISBN 0-7445-0460-0

# DUDLEY
## IN A JAM

PETER CROSS

*Text by*
*JUDY TAYLOR*

WALKER BOOKS
LONDON

It was not a good season
for nuts in Shadyhanger but
Dudley thought he had
collected enough to see him
through the winter. What he
needed now was a big, fat,
juicy plum to make some
nutty plum jam.

As Dudley's front door was rather blocked by nuts, his only way out was through the window.

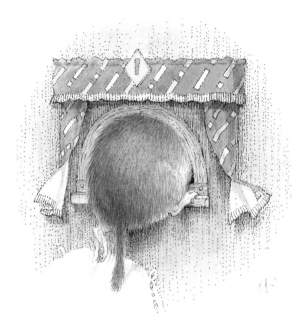

His nose twitched in anticipation
as he set off towards the wood.

By the stump of an old oak
Dudley found a pile of acorns.

'Silly to leave these for someone
else,' he thought, as he munched
his way through the lot.

A little further on he came to
the plum tree – and there on the
ground was the very last plum.

'Buzz off!' said Dudley, flicking
away a hungry wasp.

When he reached home,
Dudley dropped the
plum through
the window.

Then he started
after it, but…

Dudley had eaten
too many acorns.

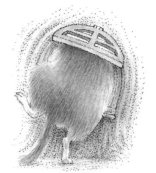

He couldn't go
forwards…

and he couldn't
go backwards.

He was completely
and definitely
stuck.

From a long way behind
him, Dudley heard
an angry buzzzZZZZZ

The sting gave him
such a shock that he
popped through the
window like a cork
from a bottle.

Dudley landed SPLAT!
right in the middle
of the ripe plum.

Though the plum was badly
squashed it would still make
good jam. Dudley put what
was left into his special
jam-making machine
and switched it on.

Dudley stirred and stirred
until his eyelids felt heavy.
The smell of the new plum jam
was delicious.

And Dudley had settled down
for his long winter sleep before the
jam had even begun to cool.